Dear Parent:

Your child's love of reading starts here!

Every child learns to read in a different way and at his or her own speed. Some go back and forth between reading levels and read favorite books again and again. Others read through each level in order. You can help your young reader improve and become more confident by encouraging his or her own interests and abilities. From books your child reads with you to the first books he or she reads alone, there are I Can Read Books for every stage of reading:

SHARED READING
Basic language, word repetition, and whimsical illustrations, ideal for sharing with your emergent reader

BEGINNING READING
Short sentences, familiar words, and simple concepts for children eager to read on their own

READING WITH HELP
Engaging stories, longer sentences, and language play for developing readers

READING ALONE
Complex plots, challenging vocabulary, and high-interest topics for the independent reader

I Can Read Books have introduced children to the joy of reading since 1957. Featuring award-winning authors and illustrators and a fabulous cast of beloved characters, I Can Read Books set the standard for beginning readers.

A lifetime of discovery begins with the magical words "I Can Read!"

Visit www.icanread.com for information
on enriching your child's reading experience.

For Emmalee
If the shoe fits, buy it!
—H.P.

For Sienna Lynne, who secretly wore
her spike heels to the mall
when she was seven!—L.A.

The art was created digitally in Adobe Photoshop®.

I Can Read® and I Can Read Book® are trademarks of HarperCollins Publishers.
Amelia Bedelia is a registered trademark of Peppermint Partners, LLC.

Library of Congress Control Number: 2020948107
ISBN 9780062961990 (paperback) | ISBN 9780062962003 (hardcover) | ISBN 9780062962010 (ebook)

20 21 22 23 24 LSCC 10 9 8 7 6 5 4 3 2 1 ❖ First Edition
Greenwillow Books

Amelia Bedelia
· Steps Out ·

by Herman Parish ❀ pictures by Lynne Avril

Greenwillow Books, *An Imprint of* HarperCollins*Publishers*

Amelia Bedelia loved to go
window shopping with her mother.
They had fun, even though
they never bought any windows.

Amelia Bedelia knew every store by heart.

There was a store
that sold books.

There was a store
that sold art supplies.

6

There was a store
for nails.

There was a shop
for nails.

Pie by the slice.

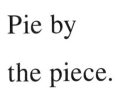

Pie by
the piece.

7

Amelia Bedelia and her mother
stopped in front of the shoe store.
"Let's go in,"
Amelia Bedelia's mother said.

BIG SALE ALL SHOES

"This is your lucky day,"

said Mr. Jenkins, the shop owner.

"We are having a two-for-one sale."

"You mean if I buy one shoe

I get the other one for free?"

said Amelia Bedelia.

Mr. Jenkins laughed.

"No, if you buy a pair of shoes,

your mother gets her pair for free."

"Amelia Bedelia needs a new pair,"
said Amelia Bedelia's mother.

"I will measure your feet,
Amelia Bedelia," said Mr. Jenkins.
"Kick off your shoes."

Amelia Bedelia's shoes went flying.

"Your feet are still growing,"
said Mr. Jenkins.
"I will be right back
with some choices."

Mr. Jenkins disappeared

into the storeroom.

"Okay, here we go,"
said Mr. Jenkins.
"Would you like
square toes?"
"No, thank you,"
said Amelia Bedelia.
"I like my toes round."

"Want to try pumps?"
said Mr. Jenkins.

16

"Not really,"
said Amelia Bedelia.
"I like my feet dry."

"How about slip-ons?"
asked Mr. Jenkins.
"No slippery shoes!"
said Amelia Bedelia.

"Flats?" said Mr. Jenkins.
"Not today!"
said Amelia Bedelia.

17

"These shoes should fit like a glove,"
said Mr. Jenkins. "Try them!"

Amelia Bedelia put her right hand

into the right shoe

and her left hand

into the left shoe.

"I don't need mittens," she said.

"I need shoes!"

CRASH!

A stack of shoeboxes fell over.

Shoes spilled across the floor.

Amelia Bedelia spotted a pair at last.

"Those shoes look great," she said.

Amelia Bedelia put them on.

She walked around.

"They fit perfectly," she said.

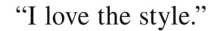

"I love the style."

"I love the color."

"I will take these!"

"I can't sell you those shoes,"
said Mr. Jenkins.

"Why not?" said Amelia Bedelia.

"Because those are your shoes!" he said.

"I can't sell you your own shoes."

"I hope not," said Amelia Bedelia.

"That would be a none-for-one sale."

Amelia Bedelia felt bad for Mr. Jenkins.

He had done his best.

Amelia Bedelia's mother

had picked out

a pair of fancy shoes for herself.

"Amelia Bedelia could use
some dressy shoes too," she said.

"I know," said Mr. Jenkins.

"What about a pair of Mary Janes?"

"Who is Mary Jane?"
said Amelia Bedelia.

Amelia Bedelia wondered why

Mary Jane would give up

a pair of her shoes.

Did she have too many?

Mr. Jenkins came back with a new box.
"These are called Mary Janes," he said.
Amelia Bedelia tried them on.

Amelia Bedelia
walked around.

"Where are your toes?"

asked her mother.

"On my feet," said Amelia Bedelia.

"Do they have room to grow?"

asked Mr. Jenkins.

Amelia Bedelia wiggled her toes.

"Yes!" she said. "Thank you!"

Amelia Bedelia asked if they could wear their fancy new shoes home.

"How about ice cream to celebrate?" Amelia Bedelia's mother said.

"Oh, goody!" said Amelia Bedelia.
"Like goody-two-shoes?"
asked Amelia Bedelia's
mother with a laugh.

"No, Mom," said Amelia Bedelia.

"We made it goody-four-shoes."